Amazing Hands

Jude Tolar

Thumbs Up 4

A Handful of Bones 6

Moving Muscles 8

Sensitive Nerves 10

Pulsing Blood Vessels 12

Secret of Your Identity 14

Index 16

Rigby

Have you ever thought about how many things your hands can do? Your hands can doodle, write, and draw. They can dig, scoop, and pat. They can toss, twirl, and catch.

Your hands can feel sharp thorns and smooth fur. They can sense pain, heat, and cold. Your hands are amazing!

Thumbs Up

Your hands can hold and move things in many different ways. A lot of things make this possible, but most of all, your thumbs.

Try to pick up a pencil and write without using your thumb. Try to tie your shoes without using your thumb. But as important as your thumb is, it is only part of your whole hand.

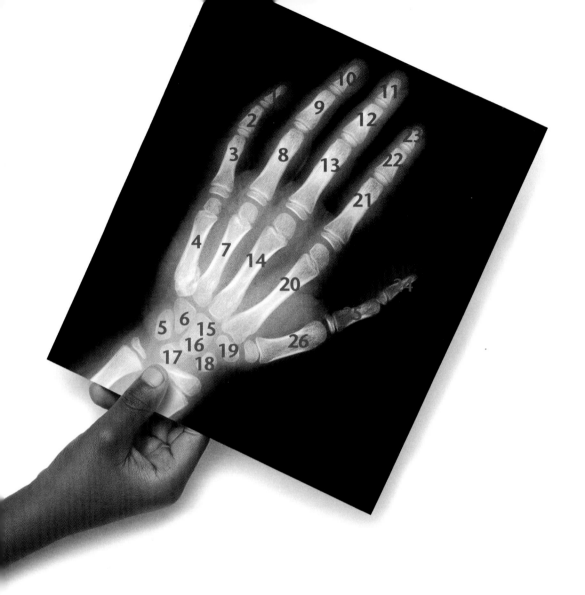

A Handful of Bones

What makes up each one of your hands? To begin with, there are 26 bones. In an adult's hand, there are 27 bones.

Seven to eight bones are in your wrist. Five bones are in your palm, and 14 bones are in your fingers and thumb. There are joints between the bones. The bones and joints help your hand move.

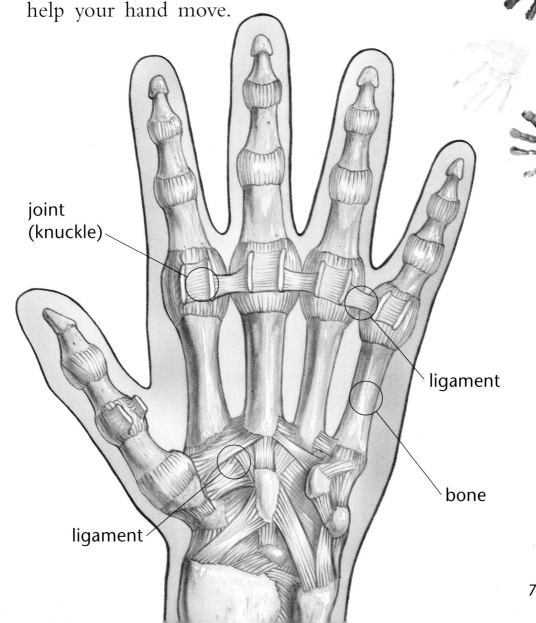

joint
(knuckle)

ligament

bone

ligament

Moving Muscles

The bones in your hand are held together by muscles and tendons. When the muscles and tendons move, they pull your bones. Touch the back of your hand as you wiggle your fingers. Can you feel some tendons move?

Your muscles allow your thumb to bend and touch your fingertips. This is your hand's most useful action. Your hand's strong muscles can grip tightly and hold gently.

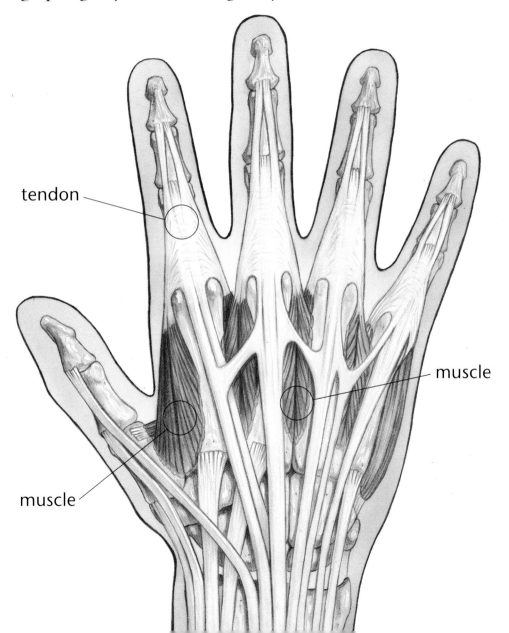

tendon

muscle

muscle

cold

hot

hard

soft

Sensitive Nerves

The nerves inside your hand carry messages to
and from your brain. Some nerves tell muscles
and tendons how and when to move. Other
nerves tell your brain what your hand feels.

You have many nerve endings in each fingertip.
This allows your fingers to feel the smallest things.
This is also why a paper cut hurts so much!

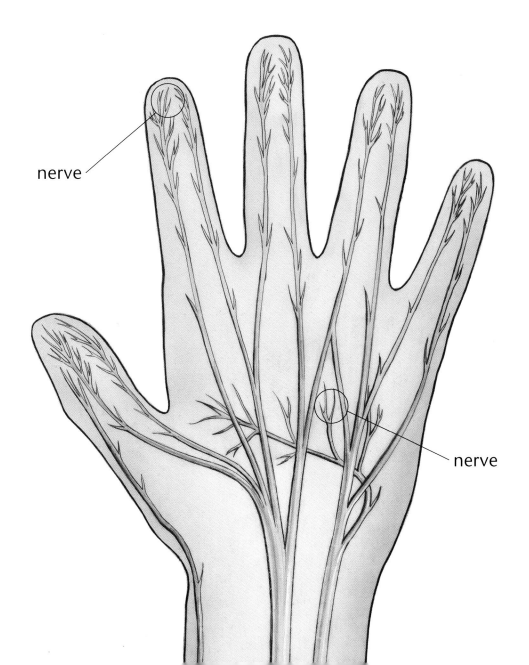

nerve

nerve

Pulsing Blood Vessels

Blood vessels are tubes inside your hand. They carry blood from your heart to your hand and back to your heart. When your heart beats, it pushes blood through your blood vessels. They stretch as blood rushes through them. The stretch is called your pulse. Can you feel your pulse at the base of your hand?

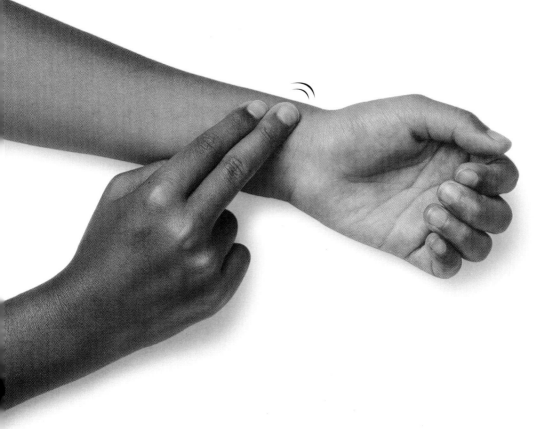

Some blood vessels look like blue lines under your skin. Can you see any blood vessels in your hand?

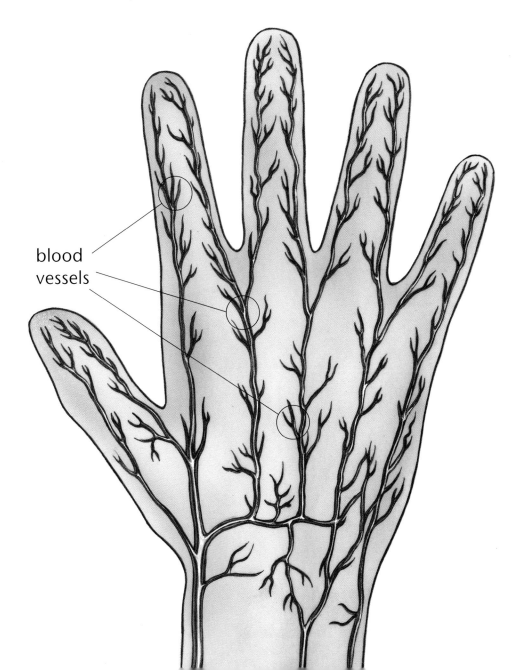

blood
vessels

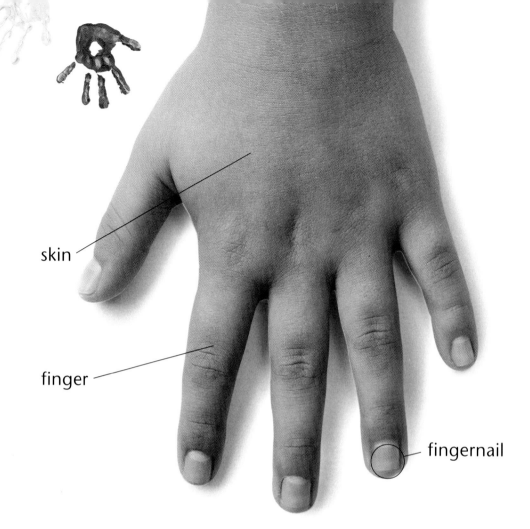

skin

finger

fingernail

Secret of Your Identity

Your skin and fingernails cover and protect all the things inside your hand. The skin on your hands holds a great secret. It is the secret to your identity. This secret is found in the ridges on each fingertip. These ridges are called your fingerprints.

Each fingerprint has one of three main patterns. No one else on Earth has fingerprints exactly like yours. Which patterns do your fingerprints have?

Aren't your hands amazing? Give your hands a hand.

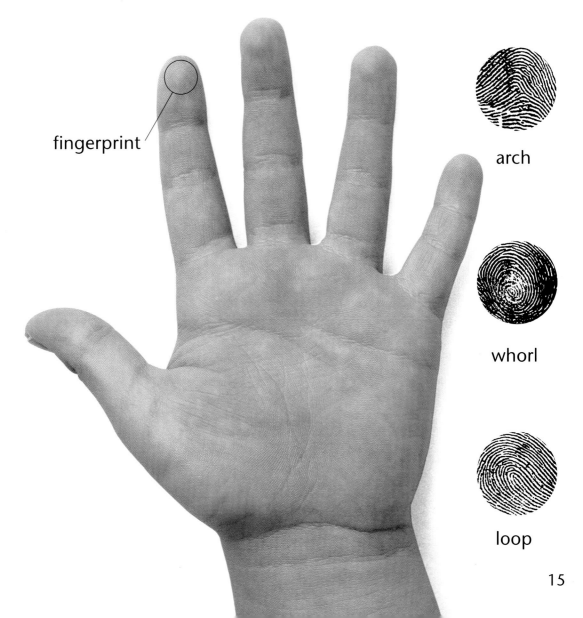

fingerprint

arch

whorl

loop

Index

blood vessels 12, 13

bones 6, 7, 8

fingernail 14

fingerprints 14, 15

fingers 7, 11, 14

joints 7

knuckle 7

ligament 7

muscles 8, 9, 10

nerves 10, 11

pulse 12

skin 14

tendons 8, 9

thumbs 4, 5, 7, 9